Library of Congress Cataloging-in-Publication Data: Brunhoff, Laurent de, 1925– The rescue of Babar / by Laurent de Brunhoff. p.   cm.   SUMMARY: With the help of her animal friends, little Isabelle rescues her father, King Babar, from the land of the lost elephants. ISBN 0-679-83897-X (trade)   [1. Elephants—Fiction. 2. Animals—Fiction.]   I. Title.   PZ7.B82843Re 1993 [E]— dc20 92-50958
Manufactured in the United States of America 10 9 8 7 6 5 4 3 2 1
Random House New York, Toronto, London, Sydney, Auckland

THE RESCUE
OF
BABAR

LAURENT DE BRUNHOFF

Random House 🏠 New York

Babar, King of the Elephants, decided to take his
youngest child, Isabelle, on a camping trip.
    They loaded the jeep with camping gear,
fishing tackle, sleeping bags, and food.
Waving good-bye to Celeste and the rest of the family,
Babar and Isabelle headed for the mountains.

At nightfall, they set up their tent and made a fire.
The night air was cold, but the fire warmed them. Babar
told Isabelle stories about brave elephants until she
fell asleep.

The next morning, they packed up their gear.
"From here we have to go on foot," said Babar.
He sent Isabelle to get water. Pretending to be
an explorer, Isabelle walked far upstream until
she found a waterfall. She filled two bottles
with cold mountain water. She couldn't wait
to show her father how well she had
done what he asked her to do.

When she returned to the camp, Babar was gone. Isabelle called, but there was no answer. "I don't like this, Papa. Please come back!" Babar didn't come back, and at first Isabelle cried.

Then she sat next to the ruins of the fire and thought. She could see that some bushes were broken. Had a wild beast been there? Had Babar been carried off against his will?

At last she said to herself, "I must rescue my father."
She picked up her backpack and set off along the trail
of broken bushes.

After walking for hours, she began to feel very tired.
She was looking for a good place to rest when she heard
a rustling in the bushes, then a roar. Out of the
underbrush sprang a lion. Isabelle took a deep breath
for courage and said, "I am going to rescue my father."
The lion replied, "In that case, I will help you.
I believe I am suited to serve as your chariot."

The lion gave Isabelle a ride. She sat on his back, holding on to his mane and bouncing as the lion loped up the mountain. Suddenly, something flew out of the trees and landed behind her. Isabelle screamed before she saw it was only a monkey.

"I am going to rescue my father," she told him.

The monkey replied, "In that case, I will help you. I have excellent vision and can be your scout."

He told her that the mountain they were climbing was an extinct volcano. "I've heard that there's a city in the crater," he added.

"Maybe my father is in that city," said Isabelle. "We have to find a way to get there."

When it grew dark,
they settled down for the night.
Isabelle lay against the lion
while the monkey did acrobatics
to cheer her up. Soon she fell
asleep.

All the next morning,
they traveled through the forest.
Isabelle was not afraid because
she had the lion and the monkey
for company.

The monkey went out
scouting and came back with
bad news. The trail of broken bushes
ended at a stone wall a mile ahead.
"How could that be?" Isabelle asked.
She decided to keep going.

The monkey traveled
through the trees while
Isabelle and the lion moved
through the brush.
In the very place where the trail disappeared,
a snake lay coiled and swaying.
"I am going to rescue my father," Isabelle said
bravely. "But the trail ends right where you're sitting."
The snake replied, "In that case, I will help you.
I know how to make the mountain open."

He wrapped himself around a little sapling and pulled until it lay flat on the ground. A door hidden in the rock swung open, revealing a tunnel.

"Follow that," he said, "to the city in the crater. But only the monkey and I can go with you. The lion would be too noticeable."

In the tunnel, the monkey and the snake kept up a constant
stream of conversation so the little elephant wouldn't be afraid.
But Isabelle wasn't afraid. The tunnel was not too dark,
since some old-fashioned lamps lit the way. And although the
ground was wet, it felt nice and cool to Isabelle after her ride
through the brush.

At the end of the tunnel,
an amazing sight greeted Isabelle. A beautiful city was built
inside the crater, with stairs and cable cars leading to the heights.

The inhabitants seemed to be elephants, but their skin was striped and they were dressed in togas. Some carried lyres, which they stroked now and then to produce lovely music.

To walk among them unnoticed, Isabelle saw that she had to have stripes. She took a Magic Marker out of her backpack and asked the monkey to draw stripes on her ears.

"With pleasure," he said. "I pride myself on my draftsmanship."

When the monkey was done, Isabelle made herself a toga out of her ground cloth. Then she looked like all the other striped elephants.

In the street, some of the striped elephants said good day to her. One of them looked at her kindly and sang a good-day song, accompanying himself on the lyre.

Coming upon an ice cream store, Isabelle realized she was hungry. She had no money, but she noticed that no one seemed to pay for the ice cream with money. Customers just sang a song and walked away. Isabelle got on line, asked for a double vanilla, and sang "Happy Birthday."

The vendor was delighted. "That's the best payment I've ever had," he said. "Will you teach me that song?"

"Gladly," replied Isabelle, and she did. Then she said, "Perhaps you can tell me where I might find the elephant without stripes?"

"I'm sorry," the vendor replied, "but I'm not important enough to know where he is being held."

Isabelle shivered. So her father was a prisoner!

Isabelle wandered through the city for many hours, looking for her father. Where were they keeping him?

She and the monkey were sitting on a bench in the center of town when she noticed a flagpole. "Climb to the top," she said, "and see if you find something that looks like a prison."

The monkey was soon back with his report:

"There's a flat grassy terrace on the side of the crater. I see an unstriped elephant who looks stuck there." "That must be the place," said Isabelle. "We'll wait until dark, then climb up to it."

By moonlight, with the snake's help, Isabelle and the monkey climbed up the side of the crater until they reached the terrace.

There was Babar, asleep in a hammock.
"Papa," Isabelle whispered. "Wake up!
It's Isabelle. I've come to rescue you."
Babar woke up. He smiled when he saw his daughter.
"I'm glad you're here," he said. "I was worried
about you. Now I can relax completely."
"What are you talking about?" said Isabelle.
"We have to get out of here, back to Celesteville."

"What for?" said Babar. "It's very pleasant here,
and the striped elephants treat me with the greatest courtesy.
Their music is enchanting, their food is delicious, and they only
want me to tell them stories. Why should I leave?"

"But you are King of the Elephants in Celesteville!"
exclaimed Isabelle.

"Let someone else be king," said Babar, and he fell back asleep.
Isabelle was stunned. What had they done to her father?

In the morning, a delegation of striped elephants came by cable car up to the terrace to visit Babar. A magnificent chorus stood before him and sang a song to greet the new day.

Isabelle stayed hidden. As she watched, a striped elephant brought Babar a pitcher of watermelon smoothie. Isabelle saw him put some powder into the glass. "Drink, King of the Unstriped Elephants," he said. "Later, you will tell us more stories about your people and their city." Then the chorus went away.

Isabelle saw what she had to do. She knocked the glass over, pretending it was an accident. Then she refilled it from the pitcher, giving her father some unpoisoned smoothie to drink.

Several hours later, Babar looked around as though he had just woken up. "What am I doing here?" he asked. "Why did you make yourself a mess with Magic Marker, Isabelle?"

Then she told him about the secret door and the magic potion, and how the lion, the monkey, and the snake had helped her.

Babar nodded thoughtfully. "I will pretend for today that nothing has changed," he said, "and tonight we will escape. Send the monkey to tell the lion to keep the door open."

Isabelle was glad to have her father back again.

That afternoon, Babar told the striped elephants the story of the building of Celesteville. They were fascinated and asked many questions. Before they left, they brought Babar another watermelon smoothie. But this time he knew better and did not drink it.

When the sun went down, Babar and Isabelle, helped by the snake, climbed down to the city.

They made their way through the deserted streets to the entrance of the tunnel.

Then they hurried through the tunnel and out the secret door to where the lion and the monkey were waiting.

Isabelle introduced her friends to Babar. He thanked them for taking such good care of his daughter and invited them back to Celesteville.

As they walked back to the camp, Babar kept looking over his shoulder. But no one followed them.

When they arrived back at Celesteville the next day, everyone was happy to see them. But no one suspected the terrible trouble Babar had been in.

After calling all the elephants together, Babar told them what had happened on his camping trip. He gave Isabelle an official medal for rescuing him and certificates of honor to the lion, the snake, and the monkey.

"The world is large," said Babar, "and it is good to see much of it and to learn of different ways of life. But for my part, I hope that at the end of my travels I will always find myself back in Celesteville."

The entire audience enjoyed Babar's talk and applauded loudly, but no one applauded louder than Isabelle.

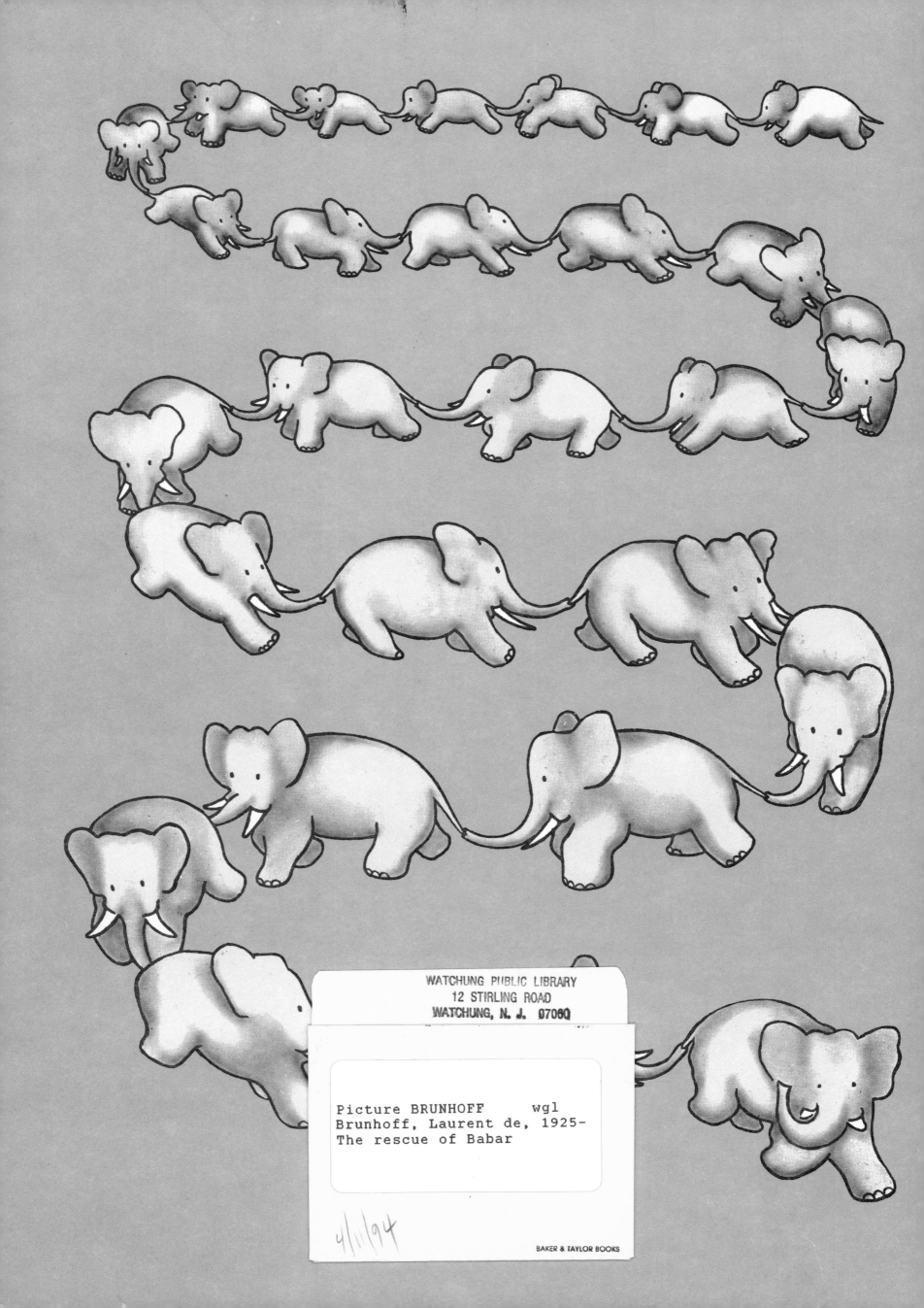